Play Me

ISBN: 9781621252665

Play Me

the STEELE BROTHERS series
book 2

JENNIFER PROBST

Dedication

Thank you to my wonderful assistant and best friend, Lisa Hamel-Soldano. You help me every day more than you can know! Smooches!

Author's Note

I've loved writing the Steele Brother series, and when I learned my rights were returned and decided to self-publish them with additional scenes, new covers, and a brand new installment, I was excited to share with my readers.

Please note these books are different from my other contemporary romance novels. The stories are erotic, with BDSM elements such as spanking, bondage, use of toys, and other explicit sexual scenes.

I never want my readers to feel disappointed, or misled, so if erotic BDSM is not your mug of tea, please do not read these books. I've decided NOT to use a pen name because my name is my brand, and I didn't want to confuse anyone. I also love writing every type of story, exploring different genres, lengths, and want to include these books under my own brand.

Thank you for listening, thank you for reading, and as always, thank you for your support. I hope you enjoy the story!

Chapter One

*H*E WAS GOING TO KILL HIS BROTHER.

Roman Steele muttered under his breath as he ended his shift, carefully checking the cards and organizing his table. He'd only been in Vegas for a few short weeks, and already his older brother was trying to run his life. First, he'd convinced him to transfer from Atlantic City, and now he'd forced him to set up a date through a matchmaking agency. Rome's temper cranked a notch. If there was one thing he didn't need help with, it was recruiting a female for company.

With methodical precision, he counted out chips and stacked decks while he brooded. The casino swung into overload as night arrived in full-blown Vegas style. The ching of the machines vibrated with noisy celebration and competed with screams of rivalry around the Roulette table. The lushness of the casino beckoned both the novice and experienced gambler to play. From the dripping crystal chandeliers, to the Merlot carpet, opulence was the buzzword of choice. Cocktail waitresses rushed by in low cut tops and short skirts with trays filled with vivid neon drinks. The familiar scents of exotic perfume, musk, and money drifted in the air. Rome held back a groan. He craved a soft bed and a hard drink. Alone. Instead, after weeks of being battered by his older brother, he'd set up this mysterious date. A date that beckoned with endless possibilities.

The perfect woman. The perfect night.

He snorted at the impossible thought. With a ridiculous name like FANTA-C, the exclusive matchmaking agency sounded like a whorehouse. But Rick was their greatest advocate. Seems he met the love of his life, Tara, through the agency and had settled into domestic bliss. Rome was damn happy for his brother, and adored Tara. But Rick was now doing what every single male succumbed to when he was hooked up into a monogamous relationship.

Turned his attention to all the other single males out there, whether they wanted love or not.

Rick had handed him a black and gold business card with the name FANTA-C scrolled in the front and a phone number on the back. He instructed him to call, using his name as the referral. Then burn the card.

Of course, being the pain in the ass brother Rome was, he asked Rick how he'd gotten a new one if Rick had been instructed to burn his original card. Seems once the date is successful, the place sends you a single business card to recruit one referral. There was no guarantee they'd find the perfect match though, so Rome figured nothing would occur, and he'd finally get his brother off his back.

Until he got the call. Guess he was the lucky winner.

Cha-ching.

Ah, hell. Maybe it wouldn't be so bad. Maybe one night with the perfect woman would get him out of his rut. Mid thirties threatened and still he hadn't found someone to challenge his dominate side. Moving to Vegas only made him more depressed as he dated the same women over and over. Chasers of money and glory. These women were out for a man to finance their dreams, or to find a cheap thrill for the night. The other category contained a tight knit cluster of friends on a weekend visit for an episode of Girls Gone Wild. If he saw one more drunken wink with the accompanied drawl of "Everything in Vegas stays in Vegas" he'd hurl.

Crap, he was becoming a grump.

He ignored the deep pang in his gut and buried it with the ease of an expert. Images of a woman by his side for the long term haunted him. His relationships always seemed to lack something crucial. Rome craved a woman who challenged him on every level—inside and outside the bedroom. He desired someone who wouldn't fear his need for dominance and surrender, but without the strict rules and limits of a classical dom/sub relationship. He shook his head at his inner whining. He needed to get the hell over himself and get himself off. He'd probably feel better.

He mentally brought up the image and three-sentence biography he'd been sent. Sloane. No last name. She looked like a stunner, and faintly familiar, but the pic had been blurry. Short dark hair. Intense type eyes. The three sentences said she was career oriented, had a strong personality, and needed a man to challenge her. Not much else was in her file to solve the clue of why they'd been set up. Wonder why--

His phone vibrated with intensity. Rome glanced down at the text.

Are you ready to meet your date?

He hesitated. Hell, what did he have to lose? A night of great sex with no strings attached. Before he could change his mind, Rome found his fingers type one simple word.

Yes.

The phone shook in his palm as if in excitement. *You will find her seated at the blackjack table, far right. Second chair from the left. Good luck.*

The screen went blank.

Rome shook his head and his phone, as the charge seemed to drop. Then with a jump, his iPhone zinged back to life. Weird. His back itched right between his shoulder blades. The same damn feeling he always got when something big was going down. Like a cheat at his table counting cards. Or a woman about to play him.

He shut down his station and headed toward Table 6. He was taking this much too seriously. Hopefully, he'll have a great night, be less cranky in the morning, and thank his older brother for the tip. No reason to bitch and look the proverbial gift horse in the mouth.

He stopped dead and stared at the woman in black at Table 6.

Her name suddenly rang through his head in a symphony of clanging bells. Sloane Keller. Champion of the World Series of Poker. "The Queen of Cards."

Rome snapped his mouth closed before he resembled a guppy. Was this a joke? An updated version of Candid Camera? He'd been half in love with her since she stumbled on the card scene with a cold confidence that pissed everyone else off. She'd come from behind and won her first poker championship with the big boys. An unknown, unnamed long shot whom everyone laughed out of the game. With icy deliberation and a talent that blew him away, she blew every other player off the table and still never batted an eyelash with victory.

Shit. She was gorgeous.

His gaze swept over her with a greediness he never experienced. The woman practically exuded "I dare you" to any guy within her distance. Her hair shimmered under the lights, an exotic black cherry that fell pin straight to brush the top of her shoulders. Longish bangs hid most of her features until she turned her head, and then he caught a whirling impression of strength. A stubborn chin. High cheekbones. Arched dark brows. Thick

5

eyelashes. Her lips were ruby red and not overly puffy like the normal Botox look that was so overdone. No, they were perfectly sculpted with just a hint of plumpness in the bottom. Her outfit added to the impression of lean power - a sleeveless black silk blouse, dark trousers, low-heeled sandals. She straddled the chair as she stared at her cards, her blood red toenails tapping on the bottom rung. Her fingers were lightning quick and her nails matched the color of her toes.

She must have sensed his stare, because her shoulders tightened and she swung her head around with a hint of annoyance.

Her gaze slammed into his with a fierceness and challenge that singed his nerve endings and his cock.

Eyes a deep violet sucked him in as deep as he imagined her wet channel would welcome him. But it wouldn't be easy. Everything about this woman screamed the need for an alpha to take her under him. Figuratively and literally.

Rome met her stare dead on and refused to look away. A few beats passed. Then she turned with a dismissive shake of her head, but he knew she was irritated she'd lost the skirmish. Satisfaction thrummed in his veins. Finally. A woman he could sink his teeth into without worrying if she'd break.

Why the hell had she signed up for a one-night stand? She had her own groupies—men who'd line up to take her to bed. She was a literal rock star in Vegas world.

He took stock of the situation. There must be a damn good reason she used FANTA-C, and he was going to find out. Obviously, she didn't give a crap he was already bought and paid for. She refused to stroll off with any man, even if she'd been the one to pursue the match. No, her deliberate action told him he'd need to earn his time with Sloane Keller.

A smile played about his lips.

Game on.

He closed the distance between them.

Chapter Two

SLOANE WATCHED THE MAN APPROACH her table with her peripheral vision and pretended to be engaged in her hand. Was this him? Hell and damnation, the man was hot. Of course, she'd met many hot men in her travels. Most of them crumbled under the personality test, but something told her he'd hold his own. In fact, maybe he'd even surpass her.

FANTA-C might have scored a home run.

He was a mixture of George Clooney and Richard Gere. Short gray hair cut close to his scalp told her he was a man who didn't give a crap he was pre-maturely gray. A sexy, scruffy beard hugged a perfectly sculpted jaw and set off the sensual curve to his bottom lip. His eyes glimmered with a controlled strength that made her wonder if he was military. The odd combination of blue and gray reminded her of rainy skies and stormy seas. He moved with a predatory grace that made a slight shiver tingle down her spine. A quick assessment confirmed his body was rock hard, evident in the thin white shirt and black pants he wore. Sloane knew from the report he worked as a dealer in the Bellagio, but spotted no nametag on his regulation uniform.

She tried to control the dip in her tummy when he stood beside her. When was the last time a man excited her at first glance? His body heat and the delicious scent of lemon and spice rose to her nostrils. Sloane kept her head down and gaze on the cards and waited for his first move.

She tapped her finger on the table for a hit. Jack of spades smiled up at her. The dealer nodded and slid the chips toward her as she met the goal of 21. Then she looked up.

He never spoke. Just waited by her side as if enjoying the game of Blackjack for pleasure. She raised her hand to her dealer, Wayne, for a short pause, and then swiveled in her stool to face the man beside her.

"Were you ever going to introduce yourself?" she asked.

He gazed at her with a bold appraisal that stripped her naked and pumped her with pleasure. An amused smile touched those carved lips. "Didn't want to break your concentration. Besides, it seems we have all night, Sloane Keller."

She raised her brow. "Perhaps. And you are?"

He seemed even more pleased at her obstinacy. They both knew she'd received his name and some brief details. Still, he answered. "Roman Steele. You can call me Rome."

He looked like a Rome. She imagined him dressed in armor and chains, leading an army of men with no thought to being disobeyed. Imagined him standing over the bed of a naked woman, ready to enjoy his spoils.

Then imagined herself as the woman. *Oh, yeah.*

As she was the only player at the table, Wayne waited patiently for her to decide whether or not she was still in. Sloane decided it was time to up the stakes. " Do you play?" she asked.

" Of course."

" What's your pleasure?" Sloane made sure she dropped her voice to a husky drawl.

He crossed his feet and bumped a hip against her chair. " Poker, of course."

Sloane wondered how he'd handle her. Most men she met either fawned like a groupie or treated her like shit. Since he was bought and paid for, she figured a bit of time before she made her final decision was acceptable. If she didn't like him, she'd demand her money back before they even hit the elevators. " Funny, me too. But I like a good game of blackjack to relax."

" Are you good?"

She smiled slowly. " I'm the best."

" Cocky, huh?"

" Confident." She leaned forward. Her lips stopped inches from his. The sizzling tension between them stretched in exquisite agony. " Not that I mind a little -- cockiness." Her gaze lingered on his lips, then dropped slowly to the evident bulge in his pants. " As long as someone can back it up."

Those misty eyes heated and sharpened like lightning. " Oh, I can back it up."

" Care to play a hand with me?"

" Thought you'd never ask." He slid on the stool next to her and motioned to Wayne to deal him in. " So, you in Vegas for business or pleasure?"

Sloane watched the cards fly and leaned back in her stool. She automatically looked for clues in his face to find what type of player he was. " Pleasure tonight. Business end of the week."

" Hitting Bobby's room, huh?"

She nodded. His casual reference held no adoration or resentment. In fact, he wasn't the least bit intimidated. A thrill shot down her spine and right between her legs, leaving her hot and wet. As "The Queen of Cards" Sloane hit the high stakes signature poker room at the Bellagio regularly. At a minimum of $20,000 to grab a seat, she believed the play was integral to honing her skill in the competition of the World Series of Poker.

Two wins placed her name at the top of the charts in Vegas. Unfortunately, most men couldn't handle the intimidation. Her last relationship bombed so badly she teetered on switching teams and going full lesbo. Not only was she physically hard up, it had been so long since she enjoyed an honest, open relationship she was afraid she'd become one of those very rich spinsters who spent their life doing things for charity. Sloane fought a shudder at the thought.

But Rome Steele didn't seem too afraid of her.

And, God, she needed an orgasm.

The thought was humiliating. She was well known in the tabloids for her exotic hook ups. Fortunately, the press had no idea they were mostly visual candy to throw people off track. Some of her most well known escorts were only good friends or gay. The ones she attempted to actually sleep with were...disappointing. Something must be wrong with her. When she did climax, it was barely a hiccup of pleasure. She craved a man's body under her hands and warming her bed, so when her friend gave her the mysterious card to FANTA-C, she decided she had nothing to lose. Sloane did not engage in one-night stands for the risk factor. This was perfectly controlled to the last detail—just the way she liked it.

Sloane pushed away her thoughts and concentrated on her hand. Ten of clubs for her. Deuce for her one night stand. She kept her head down and watched from the corner of her eye for every nuance of expression, then dug deep into her gut. Yes, he wasn't a safe player. Not stupid, but he liked risk. He'd ask for a hit fifty percent of the time when he should stay. She watched the dealer flip up an ace for himself.

She tapped her finger twice on the table. A face card stared up at her in the solemn face of the Queen. She hid a smile and put out her hand in the hold gesture. Rome's card slid across the table. Eight of hearts. A slight hesitation did him in, and his next hit revealed a six. Done.

Wayne kept his expression neutral as he dealt himself a card. Five of spades. Without much of a flicker of an eyelash, he hit himself again. Ten. Done.

The chips slid into her pile to match her first mound. Sloane waited for the fake expression of awe she usually received from her dates. Instead, she was treated to a wolfish grin that promised he'd eat her for breakfast and enjoy every last bite. Then he grasped her wrist in a firm grip and pulled her forward so their lips were inches away.

"Nice warm up. But can you do it again?"

She laughed with sheer pleasure. "Of course."

"Fine. Do it again and you get me for the night to do whatever you want with."

She gazed at him with suspicion. " I already did."

"Not yet."

Admiration cut through her. His cock, as impressive as it seemed, did not lead this man around. Curiosity teased the question from her. "What do you get if you win?"

His face turned. Determination and promise gleamed from those blue-gray eyes in warning. His voice dropped to a growl. " You, of course. But you'll listen to everything I say without any back talk." He paused and deliberately stared at her with the look of a warrior issuing an order. "And obey."

She gave him an icy glare. "Excuse me?"

"You heard me."

His commanding tone made her clench and dampen her panties. Her nipples tightened painfully, and suddenly her body was on full alert, practically begging him to make good on his threat. She forced the excitement down, knowing she'd win. She always won. Still, he never backed down, and she decided she wanted Rome Steele in her bed. Sloane licked her lips and nodded.

" Done."

Wayne dealt the cards. The stately king of diamonds winked at her. Rome took a five. The dealer turned over a lucky seven. They moved to the face down cards.

Sloane let her senses open up as her view narrowed to the dealer's hands, and the cards on the table. She looked at the next card, poised for the flip, and knew it was an ace. She watched the ace unfold and put her hand out to stay.

Rome took a ten. She knew the odds favored a bust. The man never even paused, just tapped the table. Six of spades. 21.

The dealer busted and they both raked in chips. Sloane glanced up at Rome and found no emotion etched on his face. She knew immediately he was a skilled dealer, and her respect went up a few notches. She 'd dated dealers before, hoping the knowledge and shared love of the game would be a bond. Usually, they ended up pissed off at her for winning most of the time, or became clingy when she wanted to play in other casinos.

Rome didn't look concerned or overly interested. They set themselves up for round two.

This time she hit twenty. Wayne held at 18. And her one night stand surprised her for the second time that night.

His cards added up to sixteen. Sloane prepared herself to leave the table with her winnings, cash out, and have some very good sex with her Roman warrior. Instead, he tapped the table for a hit.

If she hadn't been so used to guarding every emotional reaction, a gasp would have escaped her lips. Why would he hit? The odds were almost impossible not to bust. Her eyes widened slightly as she waited for the card.

Five of clubs.

Blackjack.

Son of a bitch.

He pulled in his chips and turned to face her. No hint of victory marred the carved lines of his face, or the steady gleam in his eye. He said a few words to Wayne and slid a few chips across the table for the tip, and then stood up and offered his hand. "Your room or mine?"

Sloane blinked up at him and tried to school her features. When was the last time she lost a hand to an amateur? The glint of purpose in his ocean eyes told her he knew her thoughts. The sudden turn of events slammed into her like a launched champagne cork.

She agreed to do anything he said.

The answering thrill hit her body as fast as her mind. She was instantly damp and pulsing, ready for him to take charge. He'd won. There's nothing she respected more in another player...or in a man.

Her voice caught on the word. " Yours."

His fingers interlaced with hers and he gently tugged her off the stool, making sure to scoop the chips in her cup. " Come with me."

15

They walked in silence to the elevators. Never spoke as the doors swooshed open on the thirty-sixth floor for the Penthouse suites. He ushered her in and clicked the door shut. She scanned the lush interior with quick dismissal, used to living in a variety of luxury hotels. The gorgeous colors of the desert theme interspersed the room with a cream sectional sofa, rich cherry wood dining area, and a wet bar that took up one whole side. The oriental carpet and watercolor canvases lent to the exclusive feel of the suite. The ceiling to floor windows gave an aerial view of the shimmering lights of Sin city during a hazy sunset.

Rome walked to the wall and hit the button. With expert grace, the blinds slowly closed and locked out the city from view, shrouding the room in a shadow. She suddenly felt like a virgin as Sloane watched him take charge. She stood rooted to the ground in a strange mixture of fear and anticipation. He closed the distance between them with a few strides.

Then smiled.

Sloane sucked in her breath at the flash of white teeth amidst the sexy stubble of beard that covered his upper lip and jaw. At the moment, she was surprised she didn't spot fangs. He looked exactly like a wolf who was about to enjoy long hours toying with his meal.

" Let's play, Sloane Keller. Take off your clothes." He leaned forward an inch so his warm breath struck her trembling lips. " Now."

Chapter Three

*R*OME TOOK IN THE SLIGHT widening of those gorgeous violet eyes and held back a chuckle. The Queen of Cards was off balance, probably for the first time in her life, and he loved every moment of it. He didn't know what was going to happen in the next few hours, but his brother had earned not just his forgiveness, but a drop-to-his-knees ass kissing. The woman in front of him called to every sense of challenge in his arsenal, and he was about to use his best weapons. She was everything he ever wanted in a woman: headstrong, confident, dominant. With a soul that cried out for a man to tame her so she could receive the ultimate in pleasure.

And he was just the man to give it to her.

Rome raised an eyebrow in question. He made sure his voice slapped her like a whip to attention. " Make me ask again and you won't like the consequences."

Heat burned her cheeks but her nipples hardened to pebbles and poked against her shirt. " Screw you."

He shook his head in mock disappointment. " I guess we'll have to do this the hard way." With deft motions, he unhooked his belt, pulled it through the loops, and grabbed her hands behind her back. Her gasp of outrage heated his blood as he tightened the leather so her hands were snugly cuffed behind her back. She immediately began to thrash and fight back, but he was quicker, and slammed her body against the wall, trapping her with his muscled build. He kicked her feet out and pressed his knee to the inside of one thigh so she remained open to him. With his free hands, he grabbed her jaw and forced her head still.

He watched her carefully for any sign of fear or panic, but her pupils dilated, and her pulse beat rapidly at the base of her neck. Lust gleamed from violet eyes, until she forced the emotion back by sheer strength of will. His cock grew long and hard in response to her obvious arousal. The lady didn't want to admit it, but she liked to play games in both the casino and the bedroom. Fortunately for him, it seemed no man before him ever had the guts to take the upper hand.

"Give me a word you'll remember."

Slight surprise flickered over her features. "Poker."

"Good. If I do something that scares you, or freaks you out, you yell poker. Then I stop. This whole night stops. Get it?"

"I'm not scared of anything."

Fierce satisfaction beat through his blood. "Then you won't want to say poker unless it's very, very necessary."

"How about fuck you?"

" Oh, you will. Soon I'll have you on your knees begging me to fuck you. Anything else to say before we begin again?"

" You son of a bitch—"

He stamped his mouth over hers. With one quick thrust, he parted those plump lips and pushed in. Hot, wet satin and the sweet taste of woman met him, mingled with the unique taste of coffee, mint, and spice. She met him full force, her tongue forcing him back in a battle he intended to win. He sucked at her lower lip, bit her, and then ravished her fully until he wrung a moan from that delicious mouth. Rome eased back, as his hands worked the buttons of her blouse. He slipped the material over her shoulders and down her arms so it hung loose around her tied wrists. One snap and the fragile lace bra fell to the ground. His thumbs moved over sensitive nipples flushed a ruby red, a perfect handful as he squeezed and massaged the tender flesh until she slumped against the wall.

"I'm going to make you come so many times you're going to beg me to stop," he whispered against her lips. He nibbled down her jaw and bit down on her ear, then blew gently. She jumped, and Rome felt the heat of her response burn between her legs. "But you have to be a good girl for me, Sloane. Can you do that?"

He watched her struggle to gain the upper hand with her mind. She pushed against him in one last desperate move to win.

The instinct to conquer and possess speared him. With a low murmur, he pushed down her black pants and dipped his head to take one hard nipple in his mouth. He laved her with his tongue and sucked while his other hand slid down the opening of her panties. Hooked under the lace fabric. And dived into home.

She cried out and arched upward. Dripping wet heat met his hand, but he made sure to give her only a taste. He traced her swollen folds while he worked at her nipple, until his name chanted in his ear to his satisfaction. Slowly, he lifted his head and removed his hand.

God, she was fucking gorgeous. Those multi-colored eyes fogged with need and a naked desire she no longer wanted to hide. Her scent rose to his nostrils and caused an animal response he'd never experienced, like a horse wanting to mount and possess in a fury of lust. But he already knew he wanted more from her and needed to pace himself.

"Are you ready to give me what I want?"

Her voice came out ragged. "Yes."

"Good. I still don't trust you so I'm leaving the belt on. I'm going to remove the rest of your clothes, and then I want you to lay on the bed with your head by the board."

Her legs shook but she obeyed this time with no delay, positioning herself on the king size bed as he requested. Rome took in every inch of her nakedness with appreciation. Long legged and slim, she was as graceful naked as she was clothed. Her nipples jutted out from perfectly formed plump breasts. Smooth golden brown skin gleamed like cocoa butter. Dark pubic curls covered her inner lips, but he spotted a flush of moisture and the nub of her clit, already heavily aroused.

Rome walked into the bathroom to snag the plush robes hanging from the hook. He grabbed two belts, and then returned to the bed. With quick motions, he unhooked the leather belt and freed her hands. Before she could say anything, he pulled her arms over her head and looped the cloth sash around her wrists to tie her neatly to the bed.

"What are you doing?"

The sharp edge of demand was back, and admiration cut through him. She'd never bore a man—always challenging him on every decision, and he loved it. "Taking away your choices."

Her brows furrowed in a frown as she tested the hold. "No. I want to touch you also. Untie me."

Rome flashed a grin at her haughty tone while she laid spread eagled on the bed. " I won the hand so we play my way. Lay back and enjoy the ride."

She kicked out one foot and struggled against her bonds. "I'm not one of your groupies. I have my own demands to make and never take a free ride."

Bingo. Sloane Keller was obviously used to calling the shots and making sure she " won" in bed, she forgot what it was like to be on the receiving end. His cock throbbed painfully against the fabric of his pants. He bet she'd fight him the whole way until he gave her the first orgasm. Rome made a quick decision. He needed her pliant so he had the time to take her in his own way.

He stripped quickly. Her eyes hungrily roved over him, but he didn't give her much time to look. He knelt on the bed and put a hand on each of her legs, gently pushing them apart until she was completely open and vulnerable.

Her breath came in huge gulps as she fought her body. "What are you doing? Didn't you hear what I said?"

"Oh, baby, I'm not giving you a free ride. But if we're going to go any further, I need you to listen better. So, I'm going to let you come and then we can start fresh."

"You bastard! Don't you dare, I refuse to come on command for you."

His eyes darkened with purpose as he lowered himself between her legs. " Let's see who wins this round."

" Roman, I -oh!"

He parted her lips and touched his tongue to her throbbing folds. Immediately a rush of liquid warmth met him at her entrance, as he gently laved her, teasing with quick licks of his tongue that never gave her the pressure she craved. She bucked underneath him, frantic to fight him and to reach orgasm. She tasted like heaven, musky and fragrant. He worked one finger in her opening and slid in and out, giving her a tiny taste of what his cock would do later on. Her cries became frenzied as she moved close to the edge, and with one swift movement, he pressed his tongue hard against her clit while he plunged three fingers in her channel in savage demand.

She screamed and convulsed around him. He cursed viciously under his breath at her open, naked response and kissed her, stroking her legs as she rode out her orgasm. Her body fell limp on the mattress, her vivid burgundy hair fanning the clean white pillows in stark contrast.

He moved up and cuddled her, massaging her arms so her muscles didn't get sore in the position. Rome didn't want to untie her yet though. Sloane was a powerful woman, and she hadn't surrendered completely to him yet.

But she would.

Chapter Four

SLOANE LAY AGAINST HIS HARD, muscled length and enjoyed his tender caresses on her skin as she floated back to earth. Dear God, what had he done to her? She'd never had such an intense orgasm before. In a matter of an hour, she'd been rebuked, tied up, and ordered around in a way she'd never thought possible.

And she liked it.

No, Sloane admitted to herself. She loved it.

The quick glimpse of his naked body showed corded arms and chest, a literal six-pack, and a huge, throbbing cock that made her mouth water. He was so tall; when he bent over the bed, she'd suddenly felt like spoils from war. He made her walk a fine edge of fear and lust, until she didn't know how to react.

In all of her past relationships, she'd never been ordered around in the bedroom. Some men tried, but one strong protest made them back off. She'd never been a non-participant in sex, yet this stranger had gotten her off in a matter of minutes and she hadn't even laid a hand on him.

He pressed a kiss to her forehead, smoothing back her hair, and Sloane had the sudden urge to cry. Disgusted by her weakness, she pushed the emotion back and made herself concentrate on conversation to keep her mind strong. "Where did you come from?"

His chest rumbled with laughter. " Atlantic City. I worked as a dealer there for years but my brother wanted me in Vegas, so he finally convinced me to move."

"Who's your brother?"

"Rick Steele."

She picked her head up. " I know Rick. He's a solid dealer. Good reputation."

"Rick was the one to convince me to call FANTA-C. Now I'm glad I did."

"Glad I can entertain you. Signed up for a good fuck, huh?"

Her jab gave her no satisfaction. He didn't even look angry, just thoughtful. This was a man who didn't lose his temper and held a fierce control. For some reason, Sloane relaxed a bit. Why did that fact make her feel...safe?

"No. I've been missing something that's hard to find. Hard to put into words, too. Sure, I wanted good sex. But I wanted a connection that went beyond the surface. Get it?"

Oh, God, she did. And that scared the shit out of her, so she did what she did best. Use snark to hide her emotions. She was a textbook case. "Not really."

His look told her he knew her game and refused to play it. Her heart pounded madly in her chest. "What were you looking for, Sloane?"

A man to make her forget she always had to be in charge. A man to cuddle her and make her feel feminine and cared for. A man to challenge her mind and make her spirit soar. Everything a woman wanted and dreamed about and everything a woman doubted she'd ever find.

"A good fuck."

In moments, he pinned her tight to the mattress, his thighs between her legs, holding her open and vulnerable. Still tied to the bed, she was helpless to fight, but she never had an impulse to say her safe word. His hard cock throbbed against her belly, and her mouth watered to taste him. His tone was a low growl of command. "We could do this easy, or hard. I ask questions, and you tell me the truth. Cause I can't stand lies."

She wiggled but he was unmovable. All those hard muscles against her softness urged her to give in. Unbelievably, she'd never been more turned on. Her pussy grew wet and swollen, and the scent of musky arousal filled the air. His smug grin only confirmed what he already knew. "I don't lie."

"Good. Tell me why you really called FANTA-C."

She huffed out an aggravated breath but gave him the round. "I moved to Vegas about a year ago since most of my work took place in tournaments around the city. I have a poker tournament this week and I needed to blow off steam. I don't usually do one-night stands, though you probably won't believe me. But I wanted company on this tour, and I wanted to be safe. FANTA-C seemed to fit the bill."

"Thank you. And I do believe you." His voice was warm and steady and she relaxed. Odd, how she almost craved to please him. She lived her life surrounded by people who bluffed and lied for a living. She'd become a master at deciphering truth from deceit. This man held a core of honesty she sensed from the moment they met. He was different. It made her want to give a bit more.

"I guess it's hard to believe such an extraordinary woman would need an outsider to keep her company," he said.

"I'm a workaholic, and I'm careful who I get involved with. I guess you could say I'm extremely picky. " She gazed into those stormy eyes and looked for her own answers. "I'd say the same about you. Looks to me like you don't need help finding company."

His lips kicked up in a smile. " I'm picky too. Haven't found what I was looking for, so my brother wanted to step in and help."

"Help get you laid?"

He loomed over her. His eyes glinted with something she couldn't name. "Help me find the one."

Naked want rose up her throat and strangled her. She pushed it back with her usual ruthlessness and made herself speak lightly. "With a talented mouth like yours, I'd say you'd find her."

"Yes. I think I will."

She squirmed under the intense heat of his stare, and then suddenly his face changed. Sensual demand gleamed from his eyes and his mouth hardened into a thin line. "I see you like when I restrain you. We'll have to experiment with other things you may like."

The words were pure warning. Her nipples twisted into hard points, begging for his mouth. Her belly clenched. "You like to play games?" she challenged.

"Oh, yes, kitten. I like to play just as hard as you." He let his meaning sink in before dragging his hard cock through her wet juices. She shuddered and bit back a moan." Ready for round two?"

The nickname caused a flash of longing to course through her. Odd. On his lips, the endearment made her feel cherished. Her heart thundered like a pack of thoroughbreds out of the gate. " I don't think—"

" I do." His mouth came down on hers with rough command. She fought back for a moment, then gave in to the delicious feeling of being conquered and forced to release control. He nibbled at her bottom lip, her jaw, while his hands massaged her breasts and his fingers tweaked her nipples to hard points. Her clit swelled and pulsed with new demand, as if her last orgasm only made her more susceptible to every lick of his tongue and touch of his fingers.

"You taste delicious," he growled, working his way down her body. " I want to know every pleasure point. Every weakness. Does this feel good?" He pinched her nipples. The quick pain shot straight to her pussy and made her wet. " Tell me," he demanded.

"Yes." She forced the words out.

"And this?" His teeth pulled and bit her sensitive nipple, laving with his tongue as his hands massaged her ass, slipping into her crack enough to feel the leaking moisture. She groaned but he made her say the word aloud.

"Yes, God, yes, more."

He slid lower, kissing her stomach, nibbling the crease of her thigh. His fingers slipped in the tangle of dark hair and combed through, then exposed her inner lips to his gaze. "Do you like me looking at your pussy?" he asked. One finger slid through the wetness "Open more for me. Wider. Yes, like that. How does that feel?"

The heat built to an excruciating agony, fogging her mind. She had no clear thought except to give Rome anything he wanted. "I like it. I feel exposed, but I like knowing you're looking at me."

" You should see how gorgeous you are. Tied up and at my mercy. All wet and pink and swollen. Begging for just a flick of my tongue to make you come against my mouth again. Do you want to come again?"

"Oh God, Roman."

"Say it. Tell me what you want or I won't give it to you."

Sloane plunged over the personal edge of rational thought and sanity and gave him the world. " Please put your cock in me. Please fuck me and make me come."

She caught a flash of a wolf smile and he reared up to gaze down at her, open and exposed for his viewing pleasure. "Good girl."

He slipped on a condom with quick motions, grasped her legs high in the air, and plunged.

Sloane sucked in her breath at the fullness of his cock taking up every inch of space. Panic hit her full force, and she struggled to back off from the pressure of him filling every inch of her body. He called her name with sharp demand, and she glanced up, panting hard, and met steel gray-blue eyes.

"You can take me. Give yourself a moment to relax, kitten."

She shook her head and bucked, but he held firm and suddenly her body softened inch by inch. Unconsciously, she lifted up to seek more of him, and he murmured in satisfaction, rubbing and plucking her breasts until she moaned for more. Slowly, he pulled out, then slid back in to the hilt, setting an easy pace that only teased the fire and didn't come close to giving her what she craved. Sloane begged for more with her eyes, and her hips and her moans, but he gave her nothing else but the torturous slow pace that kept her mercilessly at the edge of climax and moved her no closer.

Raw frustration and temper nipped at her nerve endings. With a low curse, she sunk her teeth into his shoulder since her hands were helplessly tied to the bed. He gave a low laugh, which only made her angrier.

"Isn't this what you asked me for?"

"More. Harder."

He increased his pace and pressure but her clit burned for friction. Sloane squeezed her eyes shut in sensual agony. " Damn you, Roman, give me what I want."

"All of it, kitten. Tell me."

"Fuck me hard! Take me with your cock and make me come, damnit!"

"Good girl."

He slammed into her and her heels dug into his back as she reached. Roman grasped her hips and set a demanding, bruising pace, pushing her closer, adjusting the angle so he hit her G-spot and something deep within shimmered with heat. Again. And again. And—

She came so hard she shattered in a thousand pieces with nothing to cling to but him. His hoarse shout told her he came right afterward, but her body kept milking him hard, shooting mini aftershocks through every limb. Moisture gathered behind her eyelids at the sheer release she never experienced, and Sloane wondered if she'd ever be the same again.

He slumped over her and gathered her close, this time untying her wrists from the bed and massaging her hands and fingers with loving care. A sigh of pleasure escaped her lips. When he was done, Rome pulled her firmly into his arms, surrounding her with a warmth and comfort she rarely experienced. Slowly, Sloane slid into sleep with a smile.

Chapter Four

"*H*MMM, WHAT TIME IS IT?"

He laughed. "It's Vegas, kitten. Does it matter?"

"You're right. I'm parched."

"Let me get you some water." He rose from the bed naked and made his way to the elaborate wet bar. Rome put a few cubes in a crystal glass, then poured the Pellegrino and added a slice of lemon. He brought it back to the bed and watched her gulp thirstily, then slump back into the pile of down pillows. "What did you do to me?"

He took her glass and re-filled it, then retrieved one for himself. He sat on the bed beside her, enjoying the view of her nakedness, and her plump lips sucking on the ice cube. He grew to a semi-hard state and she lifted a brow.

"Do you ever rest?"

"Not with you around. Tell me about poker."

Rome watched her face close up and wondered what had spooked her in the past. Or who. "What do you want to know?" she asked lightly.

"Not many little girls grow up to be world known poker players. How did you get involved with the business?"

He wondered if she'd tell the truth or lie. This was a woman not afraid of the truth. But in her world, hiding emotion was key to the win. Rome wondered if too many years playing the game so hard taught her to hide. She was a fierce warrior who would be forever loyal once you belonged to her. Roman wondered how many men she'd claimed, and the jealousy burned like a shot of whiskey.

"I grew up as a vagabond. My mom took off when I was young and my dad raised me. Unfortunately, my dad was a huge gambler and a con artist. He loved it all: horseracing, slots, tables. He couldn't drag me to the casinos until I was legal, but he gave me an education early."

"How so?"

She shrugged elegant shoulders and stared at the ice in her glass. "He taught me how to pickpocket. How to use my age to distract a mark. Then he got me a fake ID, dressed me up, and took me into the casinos."

The reality of her childhood struck him hard. "What about school?"

"I went here and there. Mostly, I educated myself. I was obsessed with books - all kinds. Classics, poetry, business. Then I started reading psychology and found the art of reading people. Ticks, facial expressions, how people lied. My education was the best because it was on the street." She hmphed in disdain. "Stupid people spend thousands for a degree when they could get anything they need free. Anyway, something clicked with poker. I was pretty good at math, and had a photographic memory. I also got my father's skill."

"What was that?"

She gave a twisted smile. "The luck of the Irish, of course. Unfortunately, my dad liked the drink as much as the gambling."

"What happened?"

Darkness stole over her face for a second. Then she pushed it away with an expert ease he recognized immediately. "Found him passed out in a hotel with an empty bottle at his side. Had a heart attack and died on the spot."

"How old were you?"

"Nineteen. Old enough to get by myself."

Roman nodded as if he agreed and understood. Inside, his heart stopped, and then resumed beating. "But you still weren't old enough to gamble legally."

"That's right. But I had squirreled enough money to get by. Some of my father's friends took me in and gave me shelter. And I took the time to learn." Her smile came fast and hard, with a glitter in those violet eyes. "By the time I was ready, I had made my first grand by the end of the day. It was only a matter of time before I perfected my craft and suddenly, I was sucked into the Poker circuit."

"Easy to get sucked in, but hard to remain a consistent winner."

She shrugged again and shook the ice around in her glass. "I have my father's luck. I don't drink. And I'm careful with my money."

Her will not to just endure but to thrive knocked him down like a sucker punch. She made no excuses and asked for no pity. Rome realized she used those emotions in her work. Control was key for her survival, but in the bedroom, Sloane needed to give up that control in order to feel. Somehow, some way, he knew in his gut he needed to push those buttons to go deeper.

He wanted to go deeper. But she wasn't ready. Yet.

So, he gave her what she needed. Not a shred of pity, just understanding and acceptance. "You made your life on your own damn terms." He flashed an intimate smile, and then lowered his voice to a husky purr. "Good girl."

The familiar term affected her immediately. Her pupils dilated and her heartbeat sped up. Roman scented her arousal from here, and knew she was aching and wet. He figured he had a couple of hours left before dawn.

His eyes lit on the glass she held and felt a smile curve his lips.

Sloane stopped shaking the glass. He almost laughed at the combination of wariness and lust gleaming within her eyes. With slow, deliberate motions, he reached out and plucked the glass from her fingers.

"Lay back, Sloane."

She did. She teetered on the edge of acceptance and rebellion. Roman knew she'd never bore him with her ability to keep him off balance. Her very demeanor called to his soul to complete him.

"Now, close your eyes and don't open them until I tell you."

He adjusted her on the bed with her hands up by her head to lift her breasts upward, and then pulled her knees up so her pussy was exposed to his gaze. Her eyes flew open. " What are you doing?"

He sighed. "Another direct order disobeyed."

Her eyes flashed fire. " I'm not your sub, buddy. And I like my eyes opened."

Roman left her for a moment, and then returned with a silk pillowcase. " Again, we'll do it the hard way."

" But what—"

He moved fast and bound her wrists once again to the headboard. Then rolled the silk fabric of the pillowcase into a sleek rope and placed it over her eyes, snugly tying a knot behind her head.

"Roman!"

"Our night isn't over yet, and you lost the bet. Use your safe word if you want, but if it's anything other than poker, I'm going to gag you."

Silence ensued. He smothered a laugh and sat beside her. Her body vibrated with tension, so he spent some time stroking her silky golden skin, relaxing her into a deep trust state. "Just relax, kitten, and let me pleasure you."

"But—"

"Shhhhh." He covered her mouth with his, gently playing with her tongue, and sipping at her lower lip until he coaxed a moan from her. Her muscles softened as he ran gentle caresses over her throbbing breasts, down her stomach, her arms, her legs. He massaged her feet, kneading her instep with hard motions that made her sigh with pleasure. He lulled her into a floating, aroused state, enjoying the open reaction of her body, and then took an ice cube from her glass.

He touched the cube to one of her nipples.

She shot up from the bed, but the ties held her, and he moved the ice over each hard nipple, and then took each peak into his hot mouth to suckle. When she relaxed against the heat of his mouth, he slid the cube down her belly, dipped into her navel, and coasted to her inner thighs. Rome kept his mouth busy, alternating his hot tongue with the cold ice cube, until she writhed under him, lit with arousal.

He took another ice cube from the glass and hovered over her clit. Slowly, he slid his fingers in and out of her pussy; wringing out moisture, then used his tongue to work her clit with long, hot strokes. As her hips arched for more, he quickly pressed the cube against her swollen nub.

She came apart, the orgasm wrecking her body in beautiful form. Roman quickly sheathed himself with a condom, and then slid home.

Her tight heat squeezed around him mercilessly. He plunged over and over, claiming her for his own, as he rubbed the melting cubes over her nipples, pinching them in his hands to further her arousal. With one final plunge, he came hard, and felt her clench around him in her own orgasm, and they fell together on the bed in a mingle of limbs and sweat dampened skin.

And Roman wondered if he'd ever be the same man again.

Chapter Five

"*W*HAT ARE YOU DOING?" she asked.

He replaced the receiver on the phone and walked toward the bed. Except the man didn't really walk. More like claim the space around him. He was even more powerful naked, as if he belonged in the Garden of Eden and had never taken a bite of the apple.

"Getting us some dinner. I have plans and they require energy."

Sloane stretched her sore muscles with a languid sensuality she never experienced. "I have a few games tomorrow. At least let me walk into the room with some dignity and not hobbled by too much sex."

His laugh was low and promising. Goosebumps lifted on her arms. Halfway annoyed at her quick response to a man she met hours ago; Sloane rose from the bed and went to the bathroom for a robe.

"Don't."

His voice lashed through the air. She stopped mid-flight. "Don't what?"

He closed the distance between them. "Don't put on a robe. I like you naked."

Pleasure speared her belly. She'd always felt too skinny, worried about her small breasts and her lanky height. This man made her feel like a goddess. Still, she wasn't so far along that she enjoyed walking around naked. Sloane forced a laugh. "Thanks for the complement, but I feel more comfortable with a robe on."

He smiled slowly. "I want to look at you while we eat and imagine what I'm going to do to you later. No robe." A touch of uneasiness skated down her spine, along with the familiar sizzle. God, what was wrong with her? Why did he turn her on so much with his demands and orders? Sloane raised her chin up and gave him an icy glare.

"Sorry, but I like to eat with my clothes on."

A discreet knock on the door halted the stare down. She made a hurried retreat, relieved at the interruption, and donned her luxury white spa robe, slipping her feet into matching slippers. She cursed under her breath when she found no ties - he'd made use of them, the bastard - but she wrapped it tight like a kimono and marched back out of the bathroom.

The silver table was set with white linen, sparkling china, and a bottle of chilled champagne. A solitary candle burned from the center, casting the room in romantic shadow. The scents of savory steak and herbs rose to her nostrils. Her stomach growled on cue as Rome lifted the silver dome and revealed buttery mashed potatoes, crisp green beans, and gravy. He handed her a flute of champagne alive with bubbles. Though she rarely drank, Sloane took a luxurious sip, noting the wonderful tones dancing in her mouth.

His gaze took in her appearance with obvious disapproval. Sloane readied for battle, intent on winning one round, but he waved his hand in dismissal and pulled out her chair. "I'm unhappy about your decision to disobey me, Sloane." His voice cut smooth and hot like caramel, but the warning was evident. Unease slithered in her belly. "We'll have to address that later. First, I think we both need to eat."

Since she had no intelligent comeback other than a curse, she glared at him from behind her bangs and dug in.

The meat was rare and melted in her mouth. She ate with gusto and focus, until her plate was clean.

"I see you eat like you have sex," he said in an amused tone. "No holds barred. It's nice to see that famous control slip away."

Her back stiffened. "My so-called famous control makes me an excellent gamer," she said formally. "I'm sorry if that bothers you."

Rome put down his fork and studied her. She refused to fidget and met his gaze head on, the stormy blue-gray of his eyes sucking her in like an undertow. " Your control doesn't bother me, Sloane," he said. "It's part of who you are, and got you to the top. It also got you out of the slums and kept you alive." His gaze ripped her polished surface to shreds, leaving her open and vulnerable. "Do you like being in control?"

"Of course."

He nodded. " What about your past lovers?"

"What about them?"

"Did they ever try to take away your control?"

She shrugged and kept her face expressionless. "No."

"Not one of them challenged you in the bedroom?"

Her temper flared and she snapped. "No, ok! Some tried but I threatened to cut off their balls, and they backed down. I can't help who I am, and I'm not less of a woman just because I like to call the shots. Who cares if I have a difficult time having an orgasm? It's not my fault." In sheer horror, the words stumbled out of her mouth in a terrible rush of honesty she tried to battle back. His calm questions kept coming like steady gunfire.

"Have you had trouble reaching orgasm in the past?"

"Not with myself."

Amusement flared briefly. "Have any past lovers tied you up?"

"No."

"You seemed to have no trouble reaching climax tonight," he pointed out.

She shrugged. " Like I said, it's been a while. I was probably backed up."

His eyes lit with humor but he didn't argue. "Did you like what I did to you tonight?"

"No. I only obeyed because you won the bet."

He laughed out loud and shook his head. " God, you're stubborn. Don't lie to me, Sloane. Not ever again, I warned you. Now answer the question."

She opened her mouth to tell him to go to hell, then snapped it shut. He was right. She hated liars. Her voice came out sulky. "Yes."

His approving smile filled her with happiness. "Thank you for telling me the truth."

She sipped her champagne and realized he'd gotten under her skin like Frank Sinatra's famous song. How had one lousy night begun to change the person she believed herself to be? His next words yanked the proverbial rug right from under her.

"Now, I want you to take off that robe so I can look at you."

She blinked. "I said I'm more comfortable with it on."

"Take it off."

Temper flared. She tossed her head like a stallion. "Hell, no. Get over it."

He nodded, almost pleased with her decision. "That's what I thought. Not adhering to the exact terms of the bet will force me to punish you."

Her eyes widened in shock. "Excuse me? Do you think this is the middle ages, buddy? What are you going to do - spank me?"

His lips twitched. "Actually, yes. That's exactly what I'm going to do."

A strange mixture of lustful anticipation at his dominance and pure horror mingled within her. A beat passed. Two. Then she realized he was serious and she needed to move. Quickly.

She jumped out of the seat and bolted toward the bathroom. He caught her in two seconds flat and tumbled her to the thick Merlot carpet. Sloane fought like a wildcat, with claws and feet, but he managed to rip off her robe with one quick tug. As if handling a china doll, he stripped her and pulled her over his thighs while his hands held her in place. With her ass in the air and bands of steel pinning her to the rug, she felt completely vulnerable. Panic flared.

"Let me go, you bastard!"

He chuckled, obviously enjoying her predicament. " I asked you nicely but you insist on fighting me. A little pain can sometimes elicit the greatest pleasure, Sloane. Especially with strong women who don't let themselves go."

"Fuck you."

He began stroking her naked flesh, rubbing, massaging, until a warm glow and arousal flooded her body. Fighting her reaction, she tried to wriggle but it was impossible to move. "Remember your safe word, kitten."

Then his hand came down hard on her bare ass.

The breath whooshed out of her lungs and her tender flesh stung under the slap. She cried out. He'd done it. He'd actually spanked her. She was going to kill him, tear him to pieces, sue his ass and FANTA-C for setting her up with a madman and--

Suddenly, that same hand returned to massage her stinging flesh and slipped downward. Oh, God, what was he doing? She stiffened, but that finger never hesitated. He glided over her swollen labia and pushed one finger inside her pussy. Her arousal soaked his finger on entrance, and he laughed low as he used her moisture to coat her clit and coax it to a throbbing nub. How was she so wet?

"Very nice, " he murmured in approval. "You, my gorgeous one, need a little push. The men you slept with were total assholes and completely unworthy of you."

His hand came down again, harder than the last one. This time she bit back her cry, but felt the treacherous response of her body, practically begging him to sink into her heat and take her hard. Again, his hand slid between her thighs to play. While her ass burned other parts of her burst into flames. Her nipples stabbed into the thick carpet, the cool air on her naked skin was like a gentle kiss, and Rome slipped another finger in, moving in a slow pace that completely tortured her.

"Strong women need a reason to let go. Only one with a will like yours could survive, but you took your body along for the ride. In order for you to feel completely free, you need someone to take away your ability to control."

Another slap. Then another. She bit her lip and the stringent barriers she kept around her body and heart and mind wobbled, tilted, then fell.

He thrust four fingers into her, rubbing her clit, while his other hand came down hard for one final slap.

Sloane came hard, bucking over his legs as she let herself go under the demands of another. The orgasm washed over her without mercy, and she rode it, sobbing his name. She heard the rip of a package, and then he flipped her over, spread her legs, and plunged deep.

He filled every crevice of her aching, pulsing body. Sloane shook her head and pushed at his shoulders, her last orgasm too intense to even want another. His low laugh raked across her ears as he pinned her wrists against her head.

" More. I want more."

" I can't. Roman, I can't."

His gaze seared with blue fire, forcing her to surrender it all. "You can, kitten, and you will. Give it all to me, I can take it. I want it."

He moved. Thrust after thrust, he threw her higher into the unknown. He claimed her with his mouth, tongue, cock, and fingers. Her sensitized clit burned and throbbed under the steady pressure, but he never relented, cranking up the excruciating tension. The wet slap of bodies echoed in her ears, and her walls held tight and milked him hard, until the second orgasm grabbed her and tossed her over. She flew and he was with her the whole time, his solid muscled length anchoring her to earth and to safety.

He tucked her against him, and the tears came. It was an ugly cry, ripped from her very soul, a place she rarely touched. Sloane tried to crawl like an animal needing isolation, but Rome refused, cradling her against his hard body and rocking her back and forth. He whispered comforting words, words that praised, words that leaked through the broken holes inside and healed her. Finally, her tears spent, she stayed in his arms for a long while, wondering what he had done to her.

Chapter Six

SLOANE WATCHED HER SLEEPING LOVER.
His chest rose and fell with even breaths. His face
relaxed in slumber, like a wolf napping after a long
night with his mate.

And she was his mate.

The knowledge she belonged to him vibrated in
every muscle of her body. He'd wrecked her for
anyone else. Yet, the terms of the agreement stated
one night only. Would he want to see her again? Or
was her lifestyle not suited to the future he craved?

A frown marred her face as her thoughts
jumbled. She travelled constantly. She played all
night and slept during the day. She made a ton of
money and her job required her to meet a wide
range of people, especially men. Not one of her
previous lovers could handle it.

So why did her gut whisper he was the one she'd been looking for?

There wasn't a man alive with enough balls to order her, spank her, and give her pleasure to the limit of his own. In a few hours, he made her feel precious and cared for. He made her feel like the woman she was meant to be - both inside and outside.

But love didn't happen in one night. It was a mirage, and would slip away in the cold morning light. Sloane had to remember the facts. She'd enjoy every last moment with him, but in the morning, they needed to part ways.

His eyes flew open as if he recognized her thoughts. She reached out and traced the stubble of his beard. He grabbed her hand and nipped at the pad of her finger in mock punishment. Sloane fought to keep the hope from showing on her face that morning wouldn't turn him into a pumpkin.

"I thought you were asleep."

"Not with an hour left before dawn."

She turned her head so he wouldn't glimpse any weakness." I know," she said softly. " My turn for a question. You never told me how you ended up as a dealer."

"Must be in the blood. My father dealt in Atlantic City his whole life. We grew up by the shore - good old Jersey boys. My mom brought us up as strict Catholics, which was hysterical since gambling is a sin. Surprised the church didn't catch on fire when all of her men tidied up nice on Sunday mornings." His face reflected an open affection and love when he mentioned his family.

The hunger to belong to his inner circle clawed at her gut in an effort to be freed. "My parents are retired now, and my most of my brothers have taken up the reigns."

"How many brothers do you have?" she asked curiously.

"Three. Rick, Rafe, and Remington. Remington is a dealer in AC. Rafe is in the military. We get out there for holidays and big occasions, but I think my parents are happy to finally have the house to themselves. They like to travel."

She smiled. " You sound like you have a close family."

"I had nothing to complain about. I had a solid childhood. I learned to live hard and play harder. I like money, travel, and casinos. But I love an evening in with a cold beer and my lab at my feet."

" You have a dog?"

He nodded. "Golden lab. Name's Bella. She's not as bad as Marley but close. I have a good friend who looks in on her when I'm on a long shift."

Sloane thought about coming home after a hard day to warm affection and furry loyalty. Imagined coming home to Rome to share every bit of her day. Yearning permeated every pore. "I always wanted a dog. But I'm not home enough, and I never stayed in one place for too long."

As if he spotted her secret thoughts, he studied her face, memorizing every feature and unlocking her secrets. Then he pulled her head down and kissed her.

Sweet. Deep. Complete. She sighed and gave it all back to him. He dragged her hand to his evident arousal and she squeezed. He let out a groan. His cock felt like iron coated with silk.

"You're finally going to let me touch you?"

He grinned with male satisfaction and propped himself up on the pillows. "For now."

She narrowed her eyes as her temper surged. He consistently kept her on edge, which only added to her arousal. Sloane made a vow to make him pay. He challenged her with his gaze to give her best shot.

Sloane gave a fake simper and batted her eyelashes. "May I give you pleasure, sir?"

He nodded. "Go ahead."

Bastard.

Let's see how he liked to play her way. She dropped her head over his chest and let her hair tickle his skin while she explored with her tongue. He tasted like salt, musk, and man. His muscles jumped under her hands as she massaged every inch of him, sinking her teeth into his hard belly and laughing low at his muttered curse. He grew longer and harder, pushing against her thigh in demand, but she ignored him, concentrating on other parts.

The sharp curve of his hip. The meatiness of his thigh. The flat brushed nipples surrounded by dark hair.

Her fingers coasted down his shins and she huffed her warm breath over his throbbing length. He tensed in anticipation and power surged in her blood. Finally, she was free to bestow pleasure on her own terms. With greediness, her hands cupped his balls and stroked, exploring the iron length of him, collecting the drops of moisture around his tip as she rubbed with teasing strokes up and down.

His sharp command raked over her ears. " Take me in your mouth, now."

Her pussy clenched in response and she opened her mouth to slide him in. He groaned as she took his cock deep in the back of her throat and slowly sucked. She swirled her tongue around the tip while she clenched the base of his cock with her hand. The tight squeeze thrust his hips up as he asked for more.

Excitement pulsed and pounded in her blood, and moisture dripped down her thigh. She wanted him to come in her mouth, wanted to give him the mind blowing pleasure he'd bestowed for hours, and she became frantic as she bobbed her head up and down, licking, sucking, until--

" No!" The cry ripped from her throat as he hauled her up and on top of him. She struggled to get back to her original position, but he stilled her with firm hands on her hips. "Ride me. Ride me and make me come, Sloane."

A new lust burned within, and she quickly sheathed him with a condom, parted her legs, and sunk deep.

"Rome!"

He stretched her fully. Her clit throbbed against his shaft, and she moved up and down, setting her own pace, as she matched demand for demand to make him come around her. His hands rubbed her breasts, and tugged her nipples, and she set a frantic pace, bucking, and arching her body as the delicious tension tightened harder and harder. With one last thrust, she scraped her clit against him and shattered.

Sloane cried out his name as his fingers dug into her hips with male satisfaction. She rode the wave and crashed, and he followed her right behind. The orgasm went on and on, shaking her body like a tree in a hurricane, until she collapsed against him.

His breath came in ragged gasps and stirred the tendrils of her hair. His heart thundered against her ear. A sense of completeness swept over her.

A feeling of home.

"What have you done to me?" he murmured. She didn't answer. Just let herself slide into the silky darkness, held tight by the man she was already falling for.

Chapter Seven

*T*HE RISING DAWN LEAKED from behind the blinds. Rome closed his eyes and fought with his decision. He wanted to wake her with a deep kiss and slide his cock into her wet heat. Wanted to take a shower with her and wash all that smooth skin, and then rub cocoa butter into every sore muscle. He wanted to stamp his possession on every part of her body, along with her soul.

She'd given him many gifts tonight. Her body. Her past. Her secrets. Most of the time, his heart beat steady. But in the pause between heartbeats, he realized he was falling madly in love with Sloane Keller.

Ridiculous. One night had changed him forever. But it didn't matter. He knew how he felt. He just didn't know how to convince her to give him a chance to make her feel the same.

Rome rose from the bed, donned his boxers, and sat in the red velvet chair beside the bed. His gut told him she'd fallen, too. Rome craved to push his advantage and bind her to him physically, a place she couldn't fight him. But, in the hard light of morning, he realized most women would run. Fast. He'd pushed her limits to the edge. He needed to let her go.

For a while.

Her tournament was widely publicized and held Saturday night. He had one week to convince her to stay.

Her eyes opened.

He smiled, his gaze caressing every inch of her bare skin, where he'd stroked, tasted, and pleasured. An array of emotions flickered in her violet eyes. He tracked each and every wild thought, and knew the exact moment she decided on playing it cool. Her stubbornness was oddly satisfying, even though it was used against him.

"Pumpkin time, huh?" she threw out. She sat up and deliberately stretched, pretending to be relaxed. Her tense shoulders and jerky movements confirmed she was one hot mess.

"Thought that was midnight."

"Midnight, dawn, same thing."

"Guess so. It was a hell of a night, though."

"Yep. I better get going. Lots to do today."

He steepled his fingers together, still watching her. She ducked under the sheet, suddenly shy, and grabbed for the robe draped over the chair. Rome didn't take his gaze from her as she struggled into the fabric, then grabbed her clothes and turned toward the bathroom. She hesitated. Yep, she wanted out fast, but didn't know the best way to make her exit.

"You gonna take a shower?" he asked.

"No. I need to get back to my room. Lots to do."

"So you said."

She glared. Rome hooked his foot over his ankle.

Temper lit her eyes but she kept her cool. "Are you just going to sit there?" she demanded.

"I'm going to watch you get dressed."

She let out a gasp. He watched her nipples grow hard. She tossed her hair like a pissy filly. "No, you're not. The night is over and so are the terms of the bet. It was a delightful evening but time to get back to reality. I hope you understand."

With that delightful speech, she stamped into the bathroom. Rome didn't move. A few minutes later, she came back out, dressed in her clothes from last night and looking like a woman who'd been well fucked last night.

And she had.

Sloane marched past him, grabbed her purse, and pivoted on her heel. "Well, I guess this is goodbye."

"Sloane?"

"Yes?"

He caught her scent, musky with arousal, spicy like cinnamon. Rome deliberately spoke slow, emphasizing each of his words in a calm, commanding voice.

"You will be punished for disobeying me again. This hasn't ended just because dawn came. In fact, this thing between us has barely begun."

She jerked back, her hands grasping for the door. "You—you can't talk to me like that anymore! This thing is over!"

She left, slamming the door behind her.

Rome stayed in the chair for a while, thinking over his options.

When he finally got up to leave, he was smiling.

Chapter Eight

SLOANE FINISHED THE FINAL ROUND, took
another sip of water, and scooped up her chips. She
nodded politely and smiled at the group of
onlookers crowded around the tables, trying to get a
peek of the famous players in the casino for the big
tournament. Sloane chatted casually with some of
her opponents, some of who she counted as good
friends, and fought her way down the hallway
toward the rest rooms.

God, she was tired.

And tense. So tense. These next few days were a
build-up to the most important tournament of the
year, one she was focused on winning. Each game
was like foreplay, but instead of being sated, her
body was drawn as tight as a pair of Spanx a size
too small. She wished she could drink, or smoke, or

have a fabulous, energy draining, mind-blowing orgasm.

Like last night.

Sloane shook her head in an effort to clear her mind from the image of Rome Steele. She couldn't stop thinking about him. His last words haunted her, twisting a deep-seated knot in her belly that begged for release. He was going to punish her. Rome wouldn't allow her to be tense. No, he'd wring her body dry until she was boneless, limp, and happy. He wasn't scared of her, or threatened. He just wanted to spank her, fuck her, and give her pleasure. On his terms.

God, she wanted him.

And just like that, there he was.

She skidded to a halt. Stared at him like a hungry she-wolf. He must not be working tonight. He was dressed casually, in dark washed jeans, a navy blue buttoned down shirt with the cuffs rolled up, and Italian leather shoes. His short gray hair only intensified those gorgeous eyes. He leaned against the wall, seemingly relaxed, but Sloane caught the leashed energy vibrating around him, the set of his square jaw, and the tightness of his finely sculpted lips.

Immediately, she grew wet between her thighs. Her nipples stabbed against the thin lace of her bra. Sloane gathered her composure, told her body to behave, and closed the distance between them. "Slumming?" she asked sweetly. She knew he worked at the Bellagio, but this round of initial games was being held at Wynns.

He grinned and pushed himself from the wall. He reeked of sex and attitude, the perfect combination. "Maybe. Maybe I came looking for you."

Her breath strangled in her lungs. "I can't imagine why."

"I think you do. Now, let's stop the cute banter and get some dinner."

Sloane couldn't help it. She laughed. He grinned right back at her and held out his hand.

And just like that, she was done. There was no way she could deny him. At least, a meal. Sloane told herself she could handle him and the situation. Plus, she was starved, and needed some downtime and good conversation.

"Fine. You win."

"I always do."

He ignored the roll of her eyes, grabbed her hand, and led her out of the casino. They headed to Botero, the famous steakhouse named for the Columbian artist, weaving past the long line of diners toward the redheaded hostess. Sloane watched as he worked his magic, whispering in her ear, and she nodded, grabbed two menus, and escorted them in.

Impressive.

Sloane slid into her seat, enjoying the view of the bronze sculpture of the Seated Woman, a sensuous display of lush curves and natural lines. The colorful floor unwound in bright flowers, setting off the perfectly placed fat cream columns. She placed her napkin on her lap and gave him a respected nod.

"Nice choice. No reservations needed, huh?"

Rome smiled but there was no trace of ego. Sloane sensed he didn't need to brag or play the game of who has a bigger dick. He did things to please himself. And her. He knew she liked a good steak and didn't doubt this restaurant was for her benefit. Warmth flooded through her.

"You could've gotten in just as easy," he commented, opening his menu. "You're a celebrity in this town. How much did you make last year?"

"Two million."

She braced herself for the usual reaction but he just nodded, and then looked up. His blue-gray eyes gleamed with pride. "Good girl."

Her tummy dropped to her toes. Sloane froze, hit hard with a lust so raw and violent, it speared through her and demanded he slake the thirst. He caught the look, and his eyes darkened, sweeping over her body like he owned her. Appreciated her.

Claimed her.

He carefully placed the menu down. Leaned in. "I can't stop thinking about last night."

She tried desperately to be cool, but heat seared her skin. "Me, too."

"I have a new proposition." Sloane waited for him to continue. "Spend the week with me."

Her eyes widened. "I don't want distractions."

Rome gave a husky laugh. "I watched you today. Your play was impeccable. I could also tell after several hours, your body pays a price. Your muscles are tight. Your face reflects a combination of weariness and a need to blow off some steam. I can do that for you."

"Are you volunteering to be my personal sex slave?" she shot back. The idea was outrageous. But the temptation of five nights of perfect sex with this man made her mouth water. "Sacrifice yourself for the good of the win?"

A smirk rested on those full lips. "No. But you will be."

"Be what?" she asked.

"The sacrifice. You'll be my sex slave."

"Good evening. May I get either of you a cocktail?"

Sloane fumbled for the cocktail list, then remembered she didn't drink. "Sparkling water, please," she croaked out.

"I'll have the same."

The waiter recited the specials and she waited patiently for him to finally leave. When they were alone again, Sloane lowered her voice to a hiss. "I'm no sex slave, buddy. To no man."

He waved a hand in the air, dismissing her concerns. "I'm offering what we had last night. I guarantee your pleasure. Your orgasms. If you do as I command in the bedroom. I'll fulfill your fantasies and make sure your body is primed for the tournament on Saturday."

The deal was delicious, but she couldn't accept. Could she? Sloane deliberately picked up the menu again and tried to focus. "I'm intrigued by your confidence, but will have to pass. I've been doing fine on my own now for years, without sacrificing myself as a slave to pleasure. But thanks anyway."

"As you wish. Now, what shall we order?"

Practice helped Sloane conceal her emotions, but his easy surrender pissed her off. It also suggested he had a bigger plan, because she already knew Rome never gave up. It was part of his personality, and a quality she admired herself.

Damn the man. He was just so...intriguing.

They feasted on Snake River Farms gold grade special cut steak with a coffee rub. Rare, of course. Plump, oversized prawns. Yukon whipped potatoes so well cooked they sang in her mouth. The sexual tension faded to the background and they talked. She loved being with a man who understood the business, loved Vegas, but wasn't caught up in the glittery trappings. With a sharp intellect and wicked humor, the hours passed quickly, until the bill came and she regretted the end of the evening.

She tried to split the bill with him, but he cut her that warning look and she melted. The Dom look. How did a man ordering her around turn her on so much? And why did she want to do it again?

"Are you staying at the hotel or heading to your house?" he asked her as they walked out.

"Hotel. It's easier to be on the premises this week."

"And what happens after you win?"

She gave him a cheeky grin. "I head out to AC for a bit, and then take a little time off."

"Nice. Are you tired?"

Sloane searched carefully for double meaning in his question. "Not yet."

"Good. Let's do some slots."

He grabbed her hand and dragged her to a row of machines. Big signs, flashing lights, and loud noises competed for players' attention. She laughed and shook her head when she found herself in front of Godzilla.

"No way. Slots are sacrilege. I'm a card player and this is beneath me."

Rome grabbed a red stool on the end and pulled her onto his lap. "Stop being a snob. I need some luck. I suck at slots. Besides, I love Godzilla. I want to get to the special bonus screens."

"I can't believe I'm doing this," she muttered. "If anyone sees me, I'd done. Front page news."

"Hit the button and stop whining."

He put in a twenty and she hit the button. After a few busted rounds, they finally scored three monster eggs in a row and the screen screamed and lit up. "Bonus! We got the bonus!"

"Damn, you are lucky. Go with the middle."

Sloane shook her head; finger paused on the three monster eggs that directed her to pick one. "No, never, ever pick the middle. Let's go right."

Screeches belted out from the machine, and the big Godzilla stomped onto the screen. Coins drifted across. BIG WIN.

"Oh, my God! What did we win?" Sloane jumped up and down on his lap.

"I don't know, do you think it's that sports car? The fifty grand? Wait, what? Is that it?"

The final bonus calculated to a mere fifty dollars.

"That's it?" she screeched. She jumped up from his lap. "I got excited about fifty dollars! I told you these things were ridiculous. I feel dirty. I need to go play some roulette."

"I'm sorry. But you have to admit Godzilla was super cool."

She glared at him, suspicion forming. "Did you play the maximum bet?"

Rome looked away. "Umm, let's go. We'll check out Roulette."

She blocked his exit, narrowing her gaze. "Roman Steele, answer my question. Did you or did you not play the maximum bet?"

His lips tightened in stubbornness. Blew out a breath. "Fine. I didn't. I hate playing maximum bet, that's how you lose all your money."

Her mouth dropped open. "That's how you win big! We could've won the jackpot but if you don't play all the lines, you get nothing!"

He shrugged. "Oh, well."

She placed her hands on her temples and rocked back and forth. "This is terrible. I'm never going to sleep tonight. I'll dream of lost possibilities."

"At least I got my twenty bucks back."

She stared at him. "I saw the bill. You left the waiter a thirty percent tip. You wear Italian designer clothes. You ordered a three hundred dollar steak."

"I don't like to lose on the slots."

And once again, she laughed, long and deep and hard, and her heart melted a bit more. He watched her mirth, smiling, and then his eyes turned to a steely blue, face carved in determination. Before she could recover, he backed her up into the corner, squeezed in between two slot machines.

Sloane stopped laughing.

Remaining still, she allowed him to bury his hands in her hair, holding her face. His thumbs caressed her cheeks, her jaw, her lips. His breath drifted softly over her mouth, the scent of red wine and coffee intoxicating her.

"I don't beg, kitten," he growled. His teeth nipped at her bottom lip. She shuddered, her blood heating and thickening in her veins. "I want to worship and wring a hundred orgasms from your sweet body tonight. I'll ask you one more time. Be mine for the week. Same rules apply. Say the word poker, and the whole thing is done."

The evening washed over her. He'd entranced not only her body, but also her mind, and her emotions. He made her laugh. She didn't want him to walk away and leave her to a lonely, empty bed. It was only one week. They'd enjoy each other, and she'd go to AC and back to living her life. She could experiment with this side of her that craved submission from a man who was worthy of her.

"Yes."

He kissed her. Firm, hard, possessive, it was a kiss tame enough for public, but seethed with the undercurrent of dirty, hard-core sex that was about to come. When he lifted his head, his eyes glittered with triumph.

"Your suite?"

Her voice was too wobbly to try speaking, so she nodded.

He led her back to the room.

Chapter Nine

*R*OME DID HIS BEST NOT TO rush her through the door, rip off her clothes, and fuck her mercilessly on her fluffy, king-sized bed.

Instead, he reminded himself she needed a few lessons. He was looking forward to teaching her.

They closed the door. He sensed her growing nerves, which was good. He wanted her a bit on edge. It made for a more intense experience for both of them. With deliberate casualness, he unbuttoned his sleeves and rolled the cuffs up his arms. She watched him with a mingle of fascination and wariness.

"Place your hands on the far wall there, kitten. Palms flat. Legs spread apart wide."

She stared, not moving, but Rome already saw the beginning of softening in her body, the slightly drugged look in her eyes when he spoke to her in his Dom voice.

"Why?"

"Because I said so."

Her lower lip thrust out in a sexy sulk. "Do you want me to get undressed?"

"If I wanted you to undress, I'd tell you. All you have to do is listen and obey. Easy, right?"

The sulk grew more defined. He tamped down his humor, giving her an implacable stare. Slowly, she walked across the room, her aura practically prickling with frustration from not being in control Still, she obeyed, placing her palms on the silver wall and placing her feet far apart.

Rome made sure he took his time before entering her space and stood behind her. The unknown was part of the high, the mental fuck she needed to get out of her head and into her body. Her nostrils flared slightly as she caught his scent.

He placed his hands on her shoulders, slowly rubbing the tightness from between her blades. Using the strength of his fingers, he worked her entire back, down her spine, above her ass, making sure he never picked up the pace. Finally, she was completely relaxed under his touch. Only then did he slip his arms around to her front and unbutton her black, lacy top. She sucked in a breath as the material parted and he stroked her breasts. Dragging his thumbs over her hard nipples, he tortured her through the lace of her bra until her hips began to move in tiny circles, caught up in sensual demand.

He flicked his wrist and the clasp opened. Her breasts spilled out, and the small, firm mounds were perfect for his hand. Her nipples grew long and tight, and he imagined how beautiful she'd look in nipple clamps with tiny rubies hanging from them. Enjoying the soft, smoothness of her skin, he lingered over the swell of her belly, the curve of her hip, and the valley between her breasts.

"Rome."

"No talking unless I ask you a question."

She gave a disgusted mutter but managed to hold her tongue. Rome knew it was only because she was afraid he'd stop, the little minx. God, he loved playing with her. She called to the Dom in him, creating a fire in his soul he never knew existed. Still keeping his silence, he dropped his hands to her silk trousers, tracing the line of the waistband. Cupped her pussy through the pants, dragging his open palm back and forth in a teasing foreplay that made her head slump forward and her hips arch up for more.

"You stun me, kitten," he whispered in her ear. He pressed his hard cock against her buttocks, nipping her earlobe while he continued playing through her clothes. "This body was meant to be worshipped and commanded at my will. How bad do you want to come?"

"Bad."

"Not yet. You're still owed a punishment."

Her breath whooshed out the same time he released the button on her slacks, slid the zipper down, and let the material fall at her feet.

"I don't want a punishment," she groaned.

"No talking. You're wearing a thong. I think you knew what was going to happen tonight." She seemed about to protest, and then snapped her mouth shut. "Excellent. You're learning not to lie."

Her growl was pure temper. He rode the edge by yanking her hips back and forcing her ass high in the air. He gripped the tight globes bare from her thong and dipped one finger into her dripping heat.

She hissed like a venomous snake.

"So wet. So hot. Let's deal with your punishment first, shall we? You'll get ten strikes. If you remove your hands from the wall, you earn an extra two. Do you understand?"

"Are you kidding me? This is humiliating. Punish me some other way. Ouch!"

He gave her a sharp sting on the right ass cheek. Then plunged his finger deep inside her pussy so she bucked back for more, caught on the edge between arousal and pain. "What did you say?"

"I'm sorry! Yes, I understand."

"Very nice. You're receiving this spanking because you were rude to me this morning. You also lied. Do you agree?"

He could practically hear her teeth grinding, caught between wanting to talk back and the need of her body for release. "Yes," she finally said. "I agree."

"Very good. Remember, don't remove your hands from the wall or you receive two additional strokes."

"I'm not an idiot, I understand, oh—ouch!"

He rained three sharp smacks on her left cheek, pausing to rub and stroke her ass. She moaned, settled back, and he gave her three on the right.

Harder.

Sloane jerked back, her hands flying off the wall.

"I'm sorry!" she burst out. "I won't do it again."

He clucked his tongue against the roof of his mouth, and replaced her hands on the wall. God, she was magnificent. He'd known she'd disobey at least once. Hell, he'd been counting on it.

"That's two additional ones. Lift your ass up more. That's it. Spread your legs wider."

He smelled the musky scent of her arousal and wanted to drop to his knees and feast. Instead, he kicked her legs further apart and worked two fingers into her pussy, wiggling just enough to give her a zing of pleasure. "Oh, God, I'm going to—"

"You will not come until I say so."

He gave her two more spanks, alternating cheeks, and she danced under the sting, little mewls escaping her lips. Rome was so hard, his body bordered on the edge of pain himself.

Without pause, he gave her the final four smacks, watching her ass turn a gorgeous shade of pink. His fingers thrust inside her drenched core while his thumb flicked her hard, throbbing clit.

"Come for me, kitten."

On a sob, she came, her body rocking back and forth, as the convulsions hit her. Rome didn't let her pause, continuing to stroke her, curling his fingers to hit her G-spot, and kept steady pressure on her clit.

She came again.

Her hands never left the wall.

Rome gave a vicious curse, watching her frame crumble with the force of her release, her pink ass trembling, and her head arched back in ecstasy. She was so fucking beautiful, an erotic goddess; so honest and demanding in her passion he didn't think a thousand years would be enough with her.

Rome scooped her up and placed her on the bed. Stripped off his clothes and placed a condom on the quilt. Eyes dazed, he climbed on top of her and kissed her, his tongue drinking in her sweetness, getting drunk on her flavor. Rome took his time, kissing her, biting her lips, working his way down her body to lick and suck and bite her breasts, until they were so swollen just the flick of the tip of his tongue wracked shudders from her body.

He parted her thighs and gazed at her swollen pussy. Wet, with her hard clit poking out from the hood, he lowered his head and sucked. Played. Teased. Soon, she was begging, her hands clasping his head as he fucked her with his tongue, refusing to stop and refusing to let her slide over the edge until she was a writhing, crying mess, beautiful and broken in her submission.

Finally, he donned the condom, brought her legs to hook over his shoulders, and claimed her.

Her pussy squeezed him so tight he almost came on contact. Rome fought himself back from the edge so he could drink in every expression on her face. He fucked her hard and deep, slow and steady, rocking his hips and scraping her clit with just the amount of pressure to finally break her.

"Please! Please!"

"Ask me, kitten."

"Please let me come, Rome! I need you, I need you..."

"Come."

He thrust deep inside her and she exploded.

This time, he let himself go with her, shouting her name as his hips jerked and he came. The brutal pleasure speared through him, and he milked her spasming cunt until the last drop of his semen spilled from his body.

It was a long time before he moved. Sloane lay boneless on the bed, her hair mussed, her skin flushed, the scent of their lovemaking thick on the sheets. He went to the bathroom and got a warm washcloth. Rome gently cleaned the stickiness from her thighs, washed himself, and then joined her back on the bed.

Cuddling her against his chest, she mumbled something he couldn't understand and clung to him, as giving in sleep as she was during sex.

Rome closed his eyes.

He had one week to convince her to be his.

Time to make his final bet. The bet of a lifetime.

And this time, he was playing for keeps.

Chapter Ten

SLOANE MADE HER WAY THROUGH the crowd with the ease of an expert. She made polite conversation with the bigwigs, had some laughs with some good friends, and schooled her face for the tournament. In usual form, she wore her standard attire of black, this time a high-necked black dress that fell right before her knee, with black ankle boots. No jewelry adorned her outfit, and her hair swung free, masking her face when she bent her head.

She ordered a seltzer at the bar and went to take her seat. The cameras whirred but she clicked into the zone, until the crowd was a distant murmur in the background. The clink of the ice cubes against the glass was the only sound that drifted to her ears, and suddenly she stiffened, as the memory hit full force.

Roman.

The man had a thing about ice. For the past week, he liked to surprise her with creative ways to torture and please her body with the use of extreme hot and cold. The memory of last night tumbled past her.

A hot wet tongue on her nipples. Sliding down so close to her aching pussy. Trapped from any visual stimuli and dependent on his breath and his touch to tell her what was happening next. A long slide down into heat. Then icy cold slamming her back and wrecking her defenses. Again. And again.

His fingers and mouth on her clit, teasing, stimulating. On the edge of orgasm as she waited for his next move. Then the slam of painful cold against her throbbing nub, hurtling her over the edge. Her scream told him she belonged to him.

The last week had changed her. It had started with sex. A release for her body and mind, and a way to help her win the tournament.

It had changed into real emotions and need for one man.

Roman Steele.

Between games and his work shifts, they met for a meal. Every evening, they fell into bed and played. Filthy, dirty, beautiful games. Games that freed her, broke her, and put her back together.

He forced her to share. Stories about her dad; her time on the streets. Stories about her past lovers and heartbreaks. She'd shared personal truths about her past she only shared with one other man before him. That man had rolled his eyes at her story and verbally lashed out. How could she be whining about her past when she was a millionaire? He had no patience for her or her poor little rich girl story. Afterward, Sloane locked herself back up tight and vowed to never share again.

Until Roman.

Oh, at first she fought the intimacy, but Roman was always fair, giving as much as he demanded, so she sat in fascination as he spoke about his family and brothers, the emptiness in his gut as he searched for his identity, the importance of his work and being in a high paced setting that heated his blood. He loved the jump of adrenalin, and the high stakes of betting. He adored alternative music, memory foam pillows, and the color blue. He hated vegetarians, liars, and reality TV shows.

And Sloane was in love with him.

She let the knowledge float before her, accepted it, and then let it go. This morning, when she woke up he was gone. At first, a razor slice of hurt caught her unaware, but she accepted his disappearance with a trust she never owned before. She'd told him about her ways of focusing before a tournament, the quiet place she got to inside her mind. For now, she needed the space, so she'd climbed out of bed, showered, and claimed her silence for the next few hours so she could go out there and win.

Sloane carefully set the glass down and made sure the ice didn't clink. Time to get into the zone.

Time to play.

The tournament began.

Her chips went up, and then decreased. She was always in it for the long game and liked to pace herself. When others began to tire, she became alive, hungry for the kill and the lure of the win. Her senses sharpened like an animal in the night, and she smelled blood. One facial reaction or flick of the cards could be a person's downfall. She made her way through the long hours of the play, until day blended into night and blended back again.

Her chips were up and she had one opponent left. Sloane fought to stay in the zone, but a shimmer of awareness crept up her spine like a kiss blowing in the wind. She turned her head half an inch and peeked from her peripheral vision.

Roman stood in the crowd watching her. His arms crossed against his powerful chest, hip out, and feet in a wide relaxed stance. His silver hair glimmered under the casino lights, highlighting the foggy blue-gray of his eyes. For one moment, their gazes met, locked, and delved deep.

Then he smiled.

Time stopped. That beautiful, masculine smile and the warm gleam in his gaze told her everything she wanted to know. Raw pride shimmered from every carved feature of his face. The quiet confidence in her ability, the naked emotion of possession, all told her he loved her.

Sloane turned back to her hand. Victory pulsed in her blood, and she knew her face reflected emotion for the first time in her life under the hot whirr of the camera.

And she knew she'd won.

When the chips were counted, and congratulations from the players eased, Sloane walked across the room to stand next to him.

"Good game, kitten."

A joyous smile curved her lips. "Thanks. Why'd you leave?"

He reached out a finger and trailed it down her cheek. " You need to get in the zone. I would have just made you a bowl of mush with too many orgasms. I respect you."

"I know."

"I also love you."

Sloane sighed. "I know. I happen to love you, too."

He laughed, shaking his head. "Good. So, here's what we're going to do."

She raised one brow. "Being bossy again, huh?"

He sighed with deep regret. " Why do you have to make everything difficult? Thank God I already have the necessary equipment to tame you."

She stared at him with suspicion. "Equipment?"

"Handcuffs, blindfolds, whips, etc. So, here's what we're going to do. I'm going to cheer you on every step of the way while you make a shitload of money. I'd like to come to Atlantic City and watch you play. I can get the time off and we can visit my parents."

"Sounds fair."

"Then you're going to move in with me."

She raised her chin. " I like my place better. You move in with me."

"We'll argue about which place is better later. In the meantime, you need some food and water and relaxation."

"You don't always know what I need, Mr. Roman Warrior. I had a hell of a day and I'll tell you what I need."

"Go ahead."

She raised herself on tiptoe and spoke right against his lips. "I need an orgasm. So get your ass back up to my room and take care of it."

His eyes heated with warning. A thrill raced down her spine.

"Good girl." He lowered his head and kissed her deeply. "Let's play."

Finally, Sloane thought as she gazed up at the man she loved.

A happy ending at last.

The End

Jennifer's Playlist

Wonderland – Taylor Swift

Downtown – Macklemore & Ryan Lewis

Animals – Maroon 5

Gett Off - Prince

I Know You – Skylar Grey

Heaven Help Me – Rob Thomas

Want tovWant Me -

Good For You – Selena Gomez

Use Somebody – Kings of Leon

Wild Wild Love - Pitbull

About the Author

Jennifer Probst is the New York Times, USA Today, and Wall Street Journal bestselling author of both sexy and erotic contemporary romance. She was thrilled her novel, The Marriage Bargain, was the #6 Bestselling Book on Amazon for 2012. Her first children's book, Buffy and the Carrot, was co-written with her 12 year old niece, and her short story, "A Life Worth Living" chronicles the life of a shelter dog. She makes her home in New York with her sons, husband, two rescue dogs, and a house that never seems to be clean. She loves hearing from all readers! Stop by her website at http://www.jenniferprobst.com for all her upcoming releases, news and street team information.

27545394R00058

Made in the USA
San Bernardino, CA
14 December 2015